Another Happy Tale

For Cushla
DB
For Jane
JH

First American edition published 1991 by
Crocodile Books, USA
An imprint of Interlink Publishing Group, Inc.
99 Seventh Avenue ● Brooklyn, New York 11215

Text © Dorothy Butler 1991
Illustrations © John Hurford 1991

Library of Congress Cataloging-in-Publication Data

Butler, Dorothy, 1925-
Another happy tale / Dorothy Butler ; pictures by John Hurford. —
1st American ed.
p. cm.
Summary: Happily, Mabel and Ned are the parents of a new baby, bu
unhappily, they are not good at taking care of her. And thus begins
a tale.
ISBN 0-940793-88-1
[1. Babies-Fiction.] I. Hurford, John, ill. II. Title.
PZ7.B976An 1991
          [E]—dc20
          91-23133
          CIP
          AC

Printed and bound in Hong Kong

Another Happy Tale

Dorothy Butler

Pictures by John Hurford

Crocodile Books, USA

NEW YORK

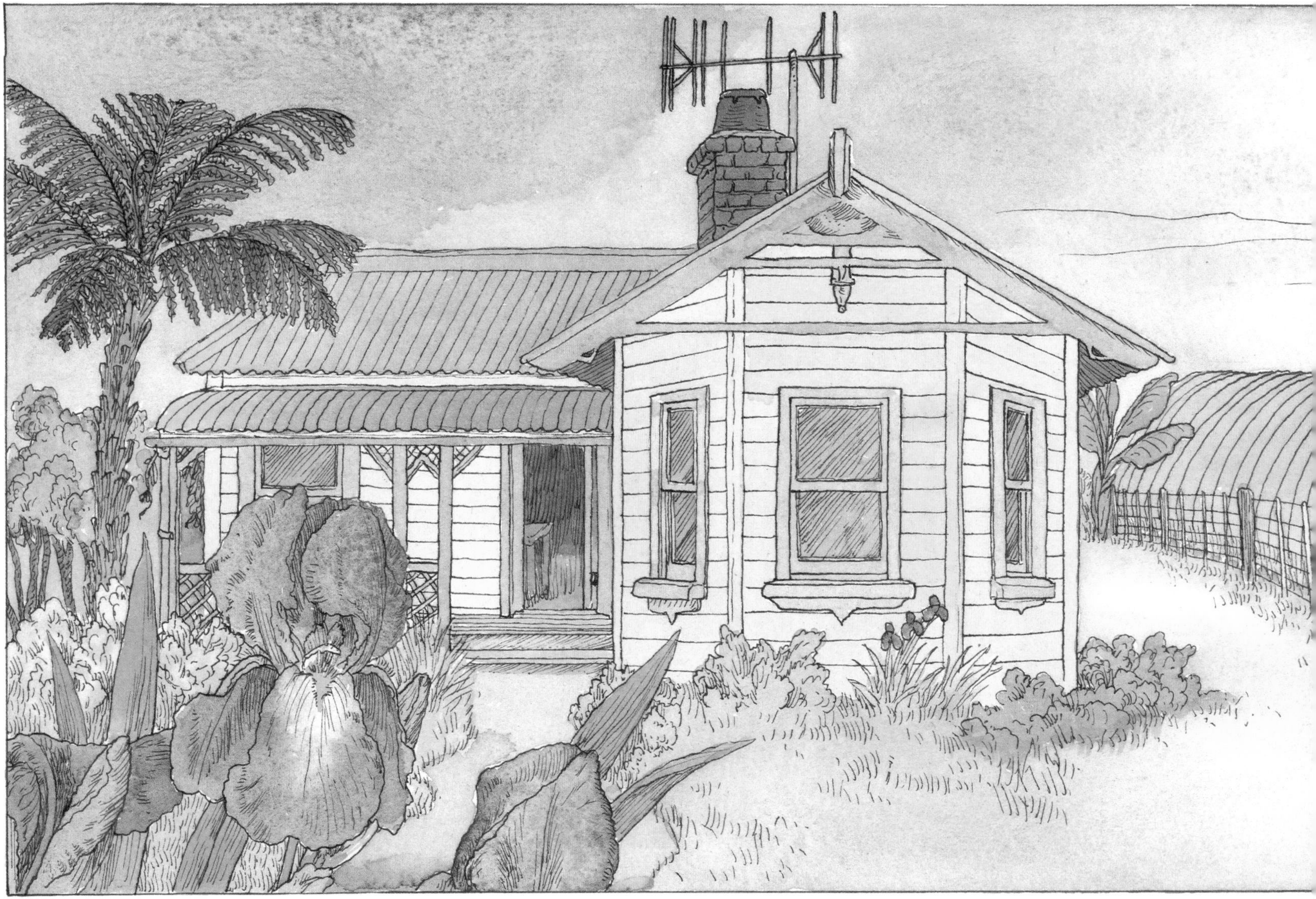

Mabel and Ned lived with their new baby on a fine farm in the middle of a large island.

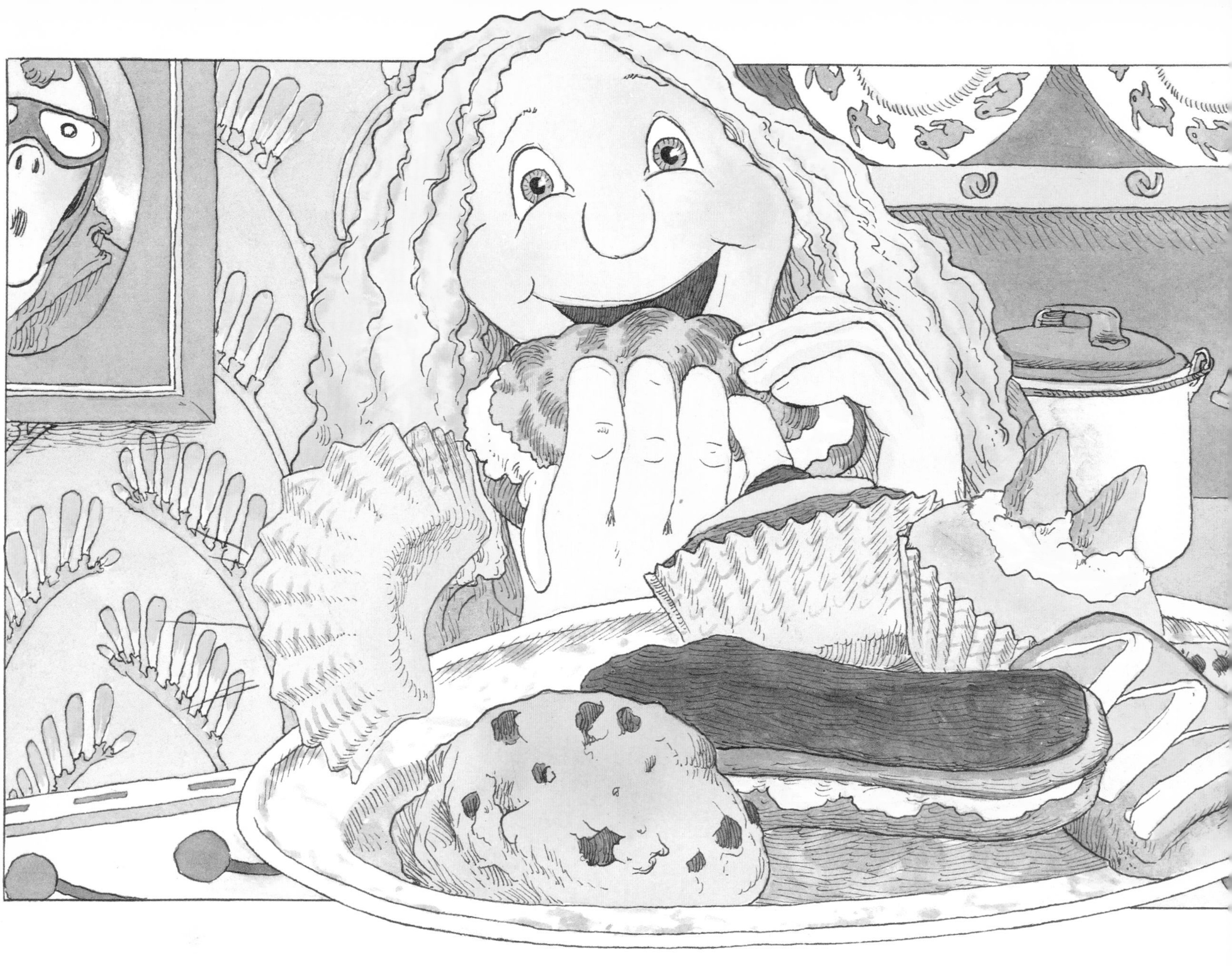

Unhappily, Mabel was not very good at looking after babies.

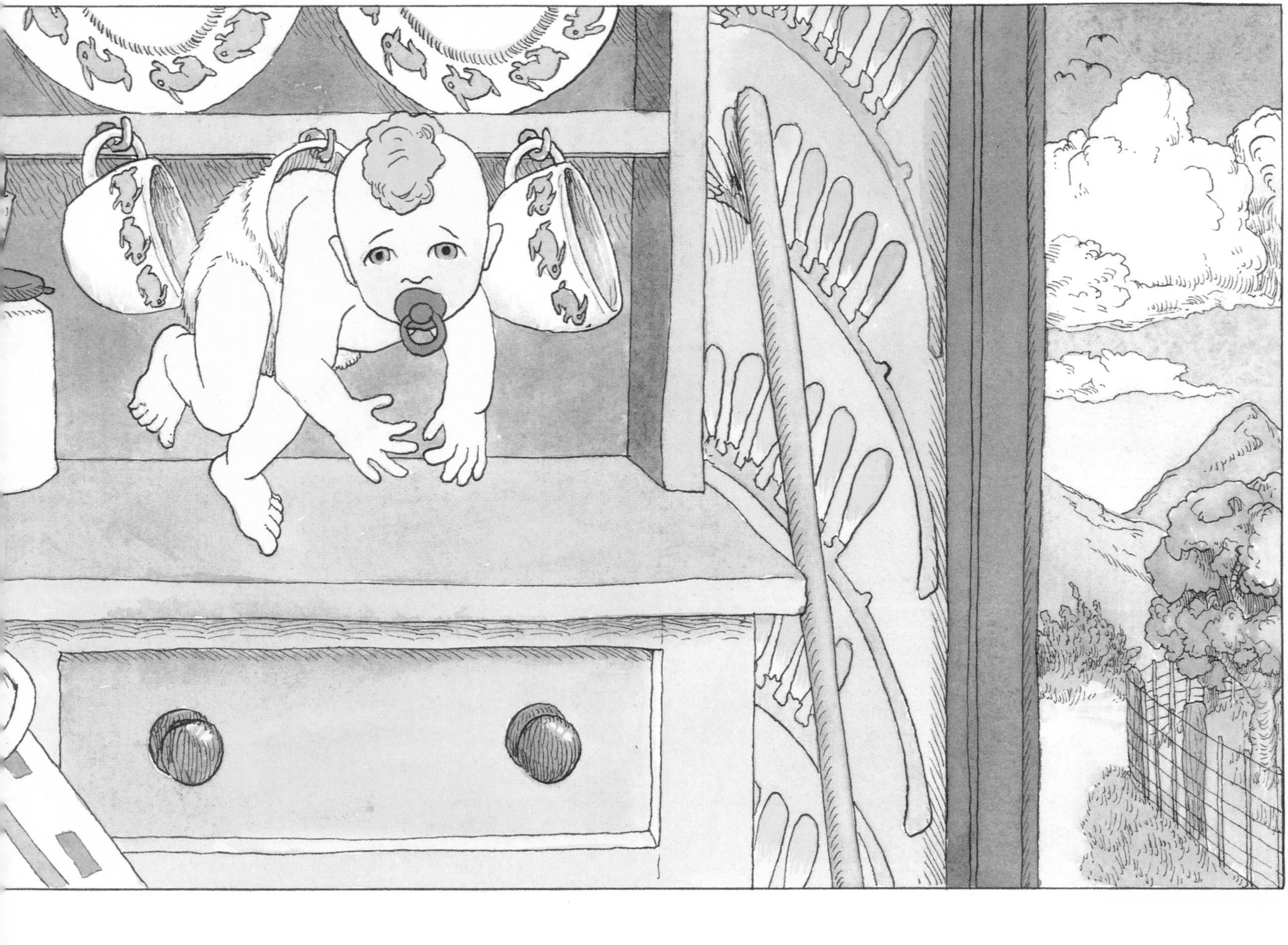

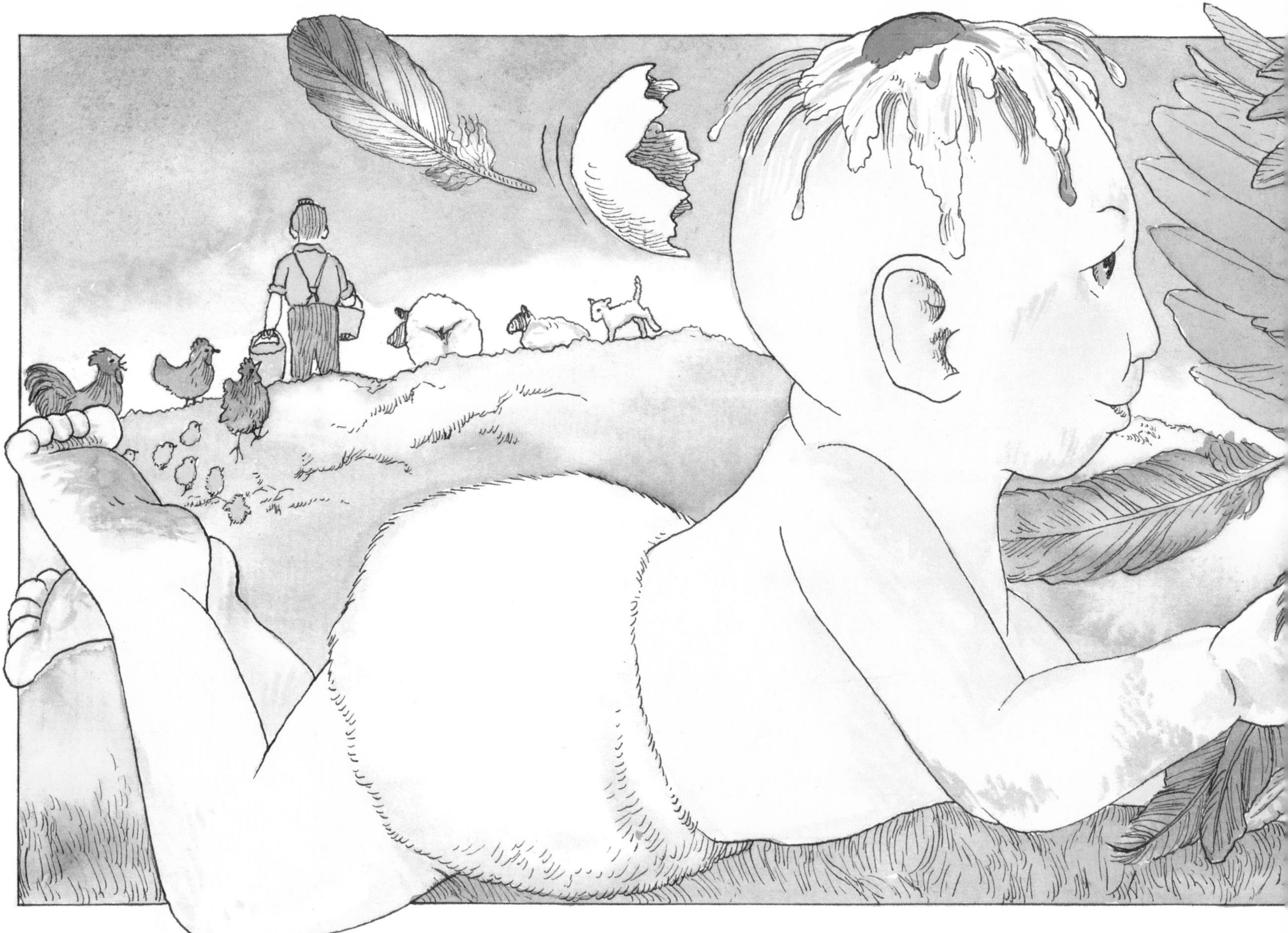

Happily, Ned, who was very good at looking after animals, said that he woul
look after the baby too.

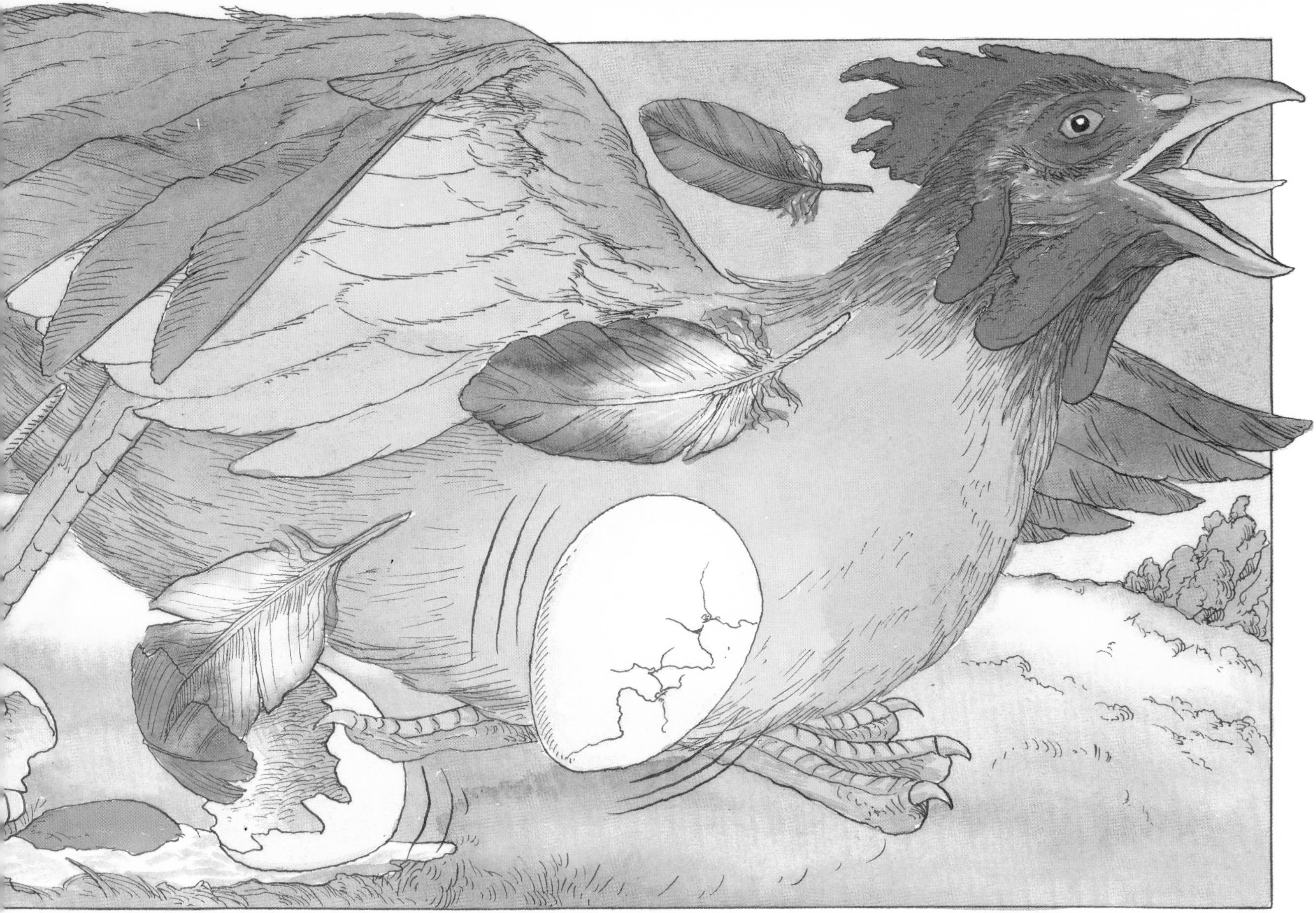

Unhappily, it turned out that Ned was not very good at looking after babies either. He expected her to look after herself, like the baby sheep and pigs.

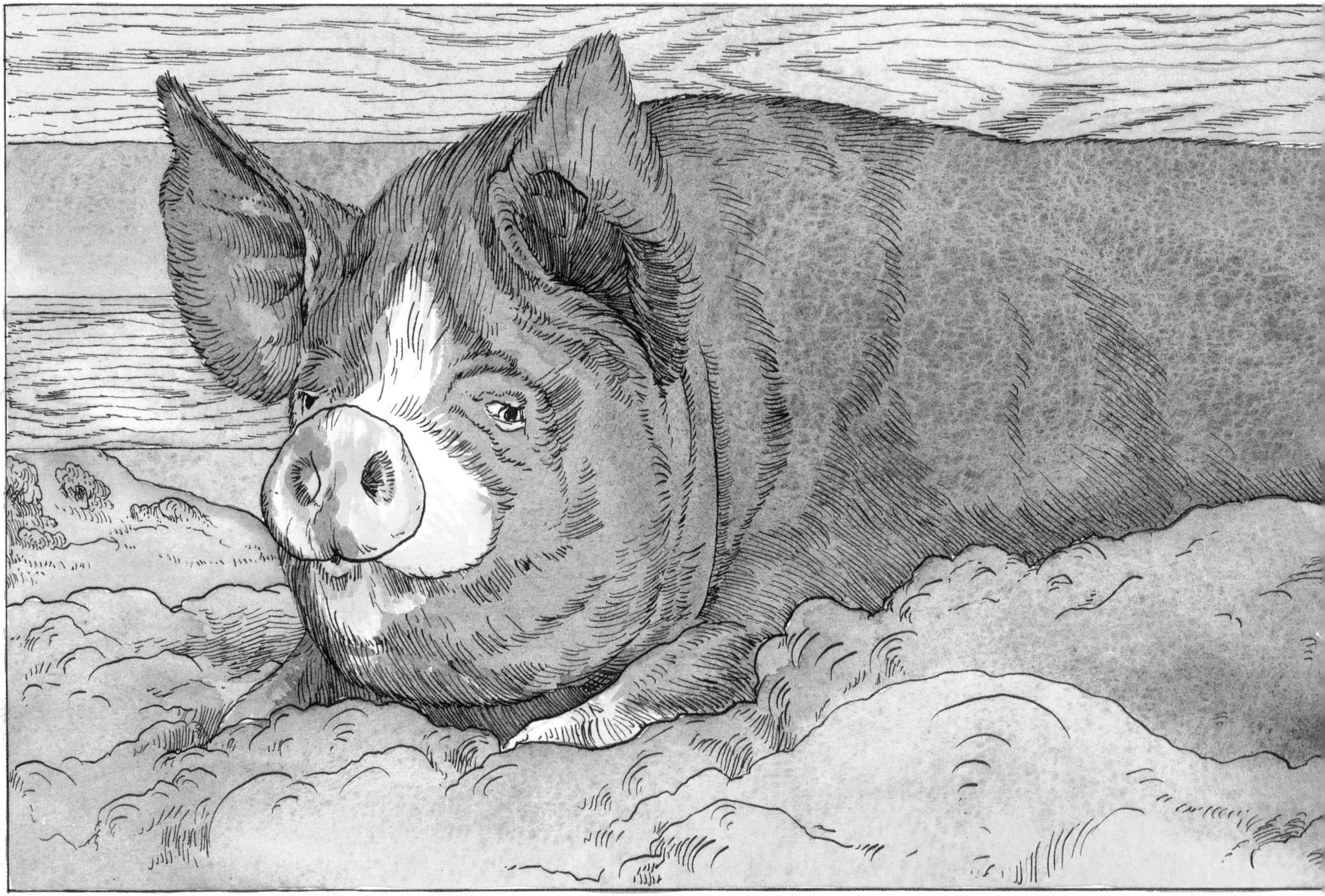

Happily, the baby turned out to be very good at looking after herself. She was especially fond of the pigs.

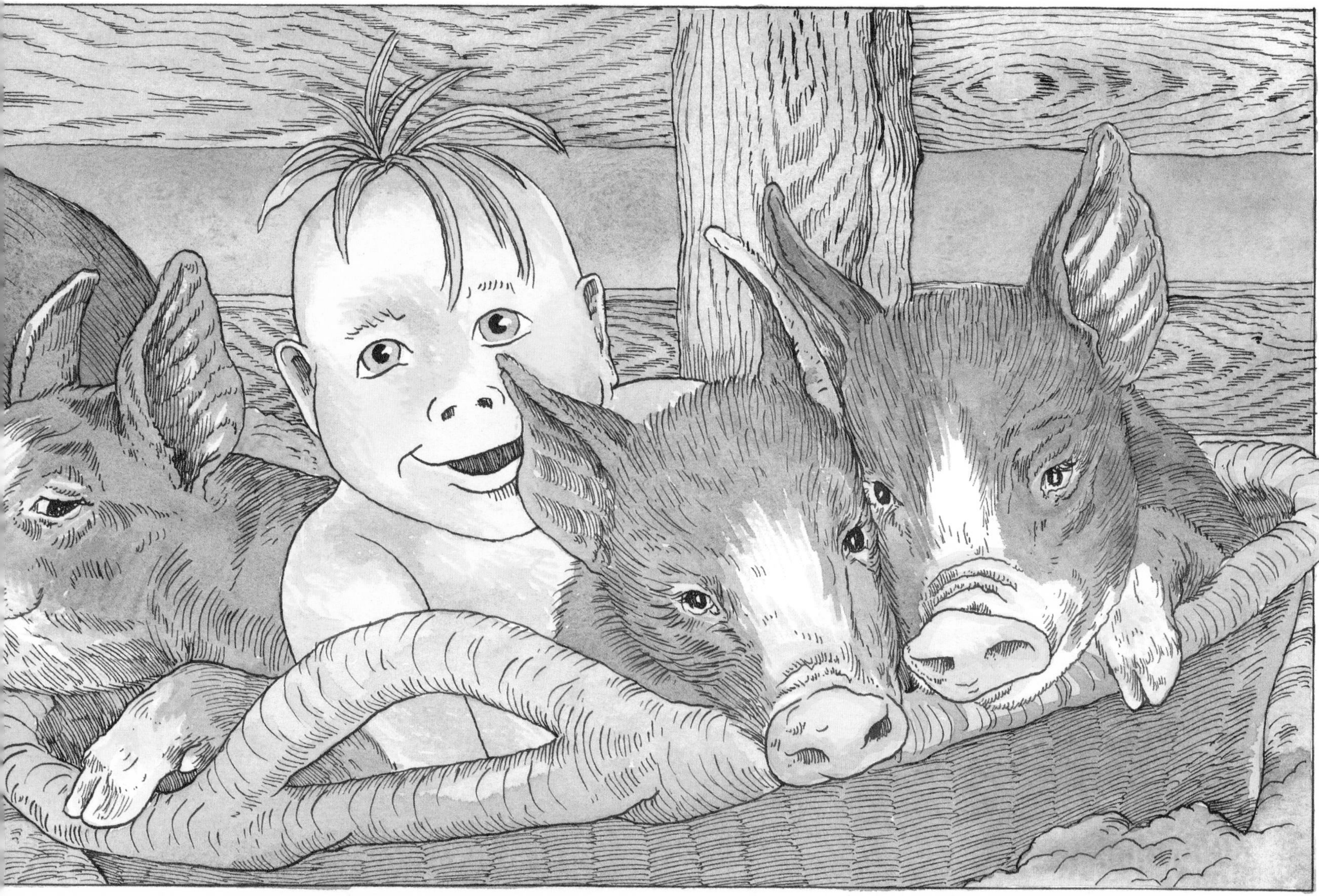

Unhappily, the baby started looking and smelling like a piglet.

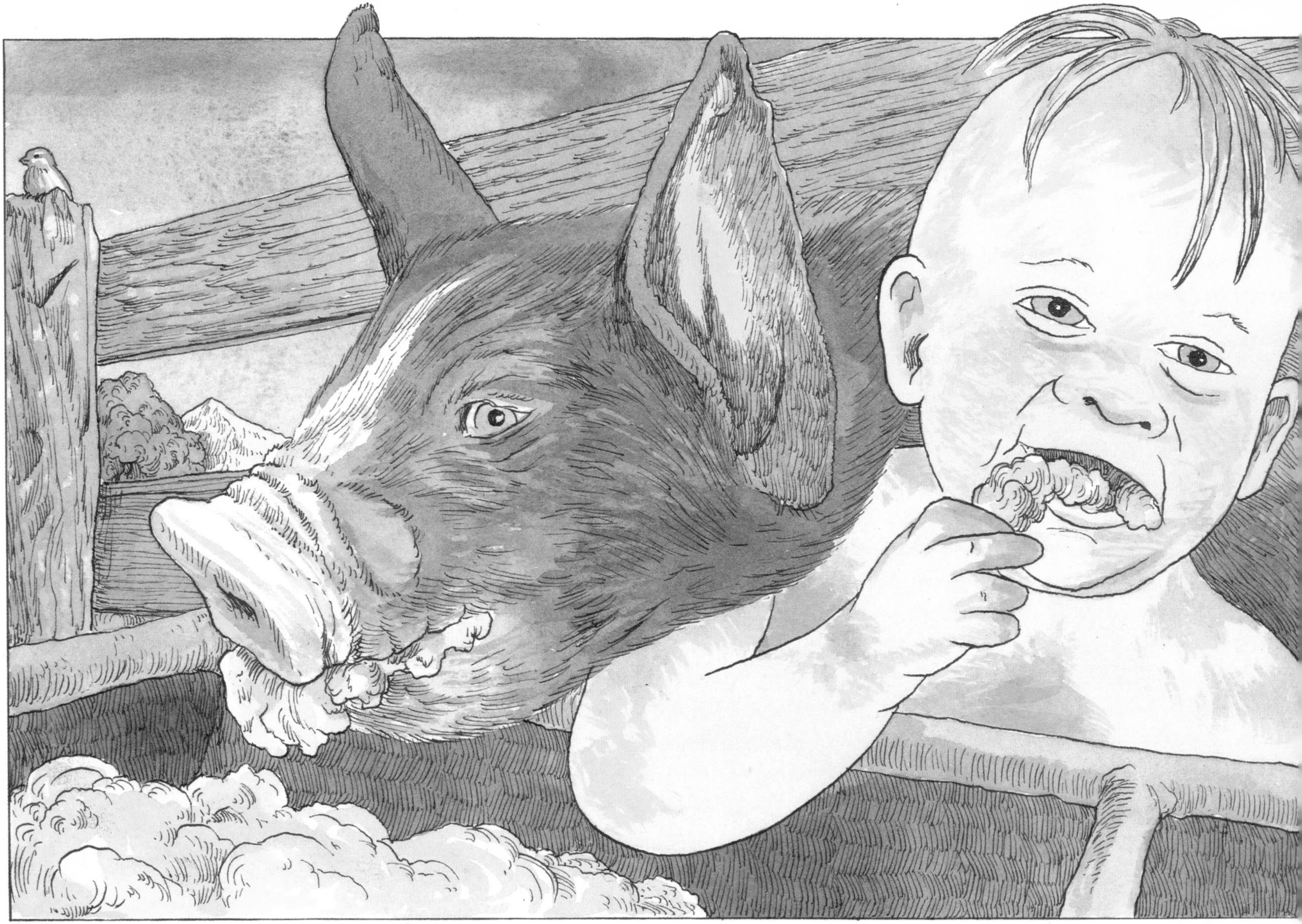

Happily, she grew to be just as fat and healthy as the baby pigs — but just as muddy.

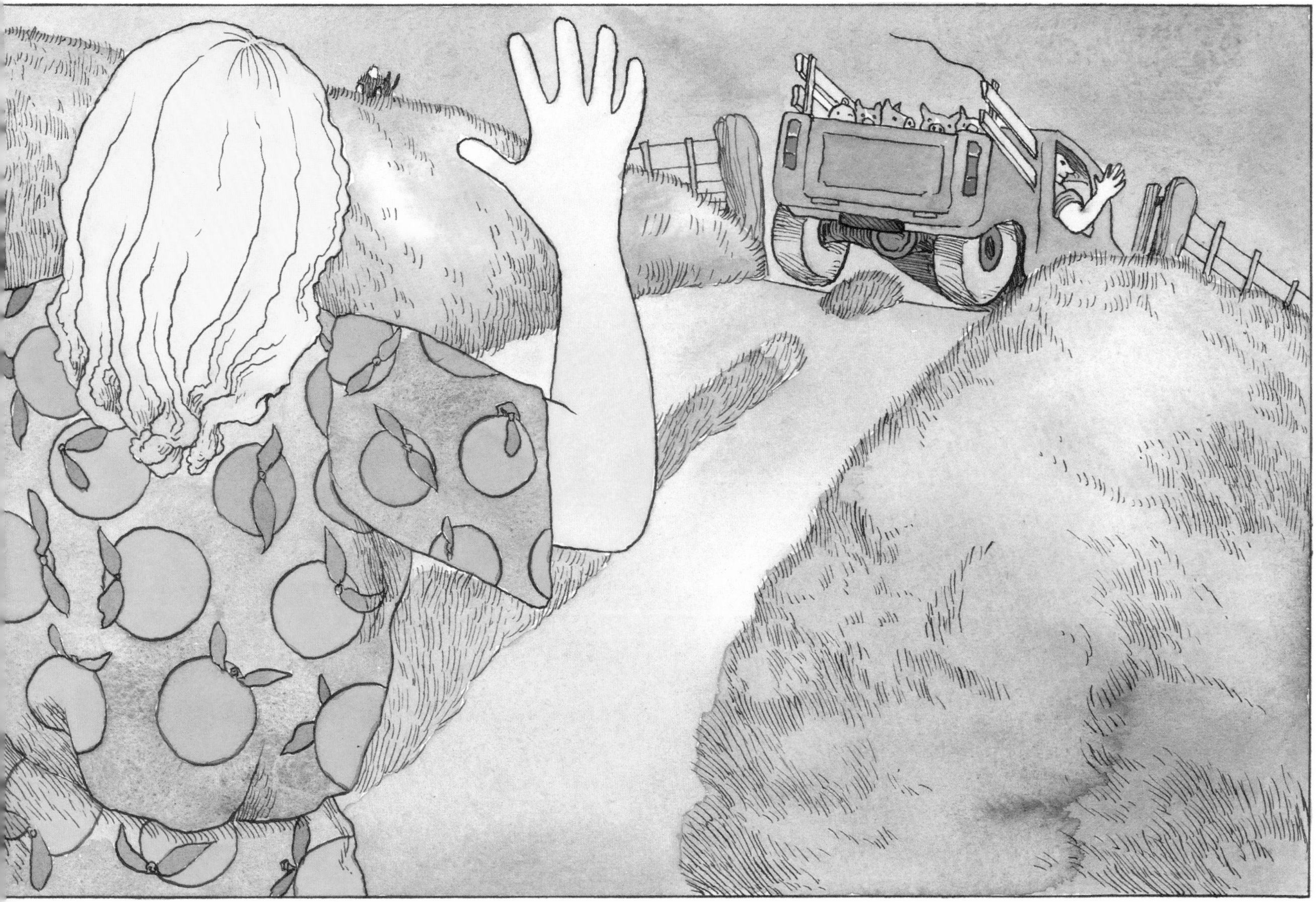

Unhappily, one day Ned rounded up all the young pigs, baby and all, and took them to market to be sold.

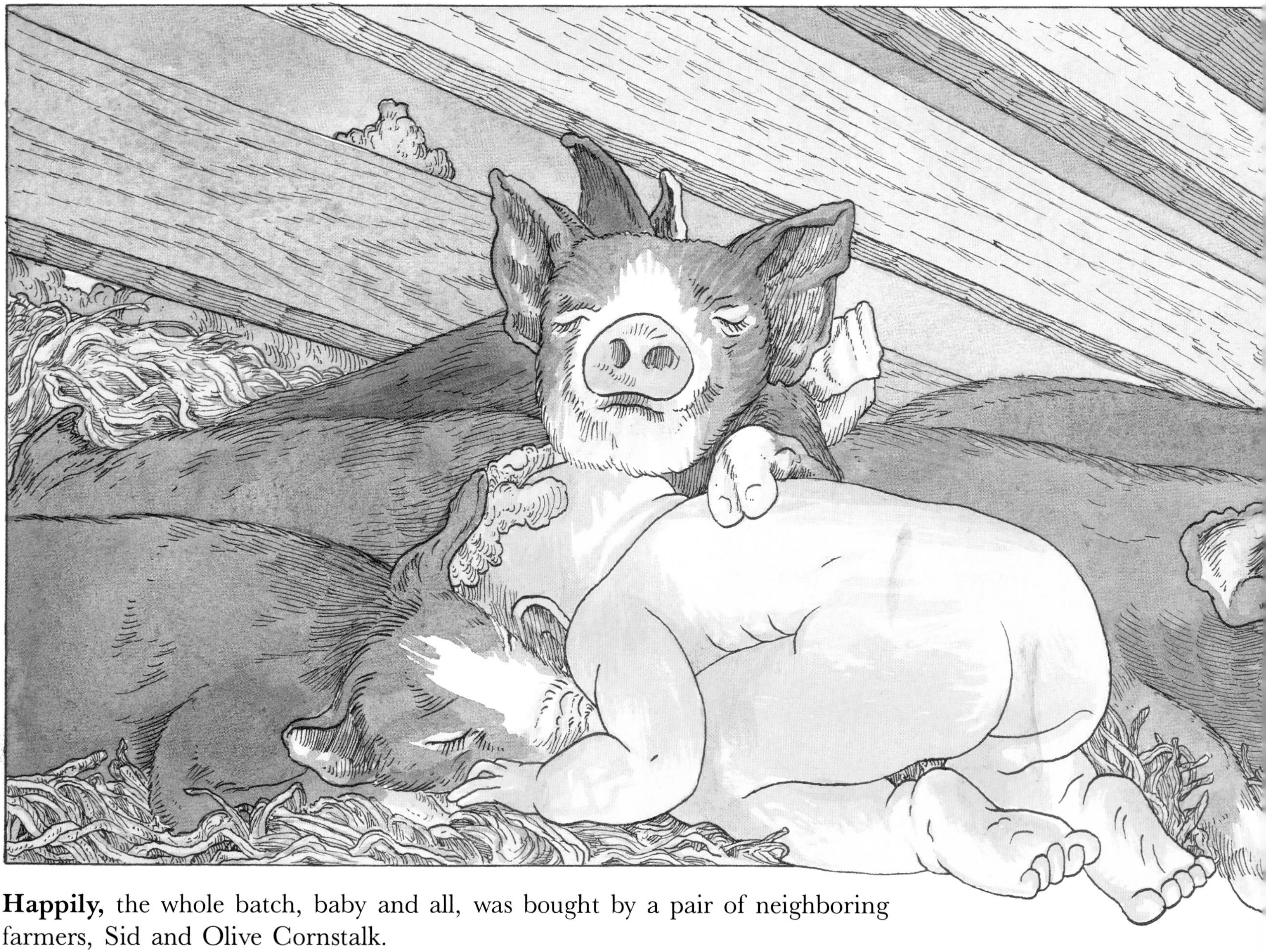

Happily, the whole batch, baby and all, was bought by a pair of neighboring farmers, Sid and Olive Cornstalk.

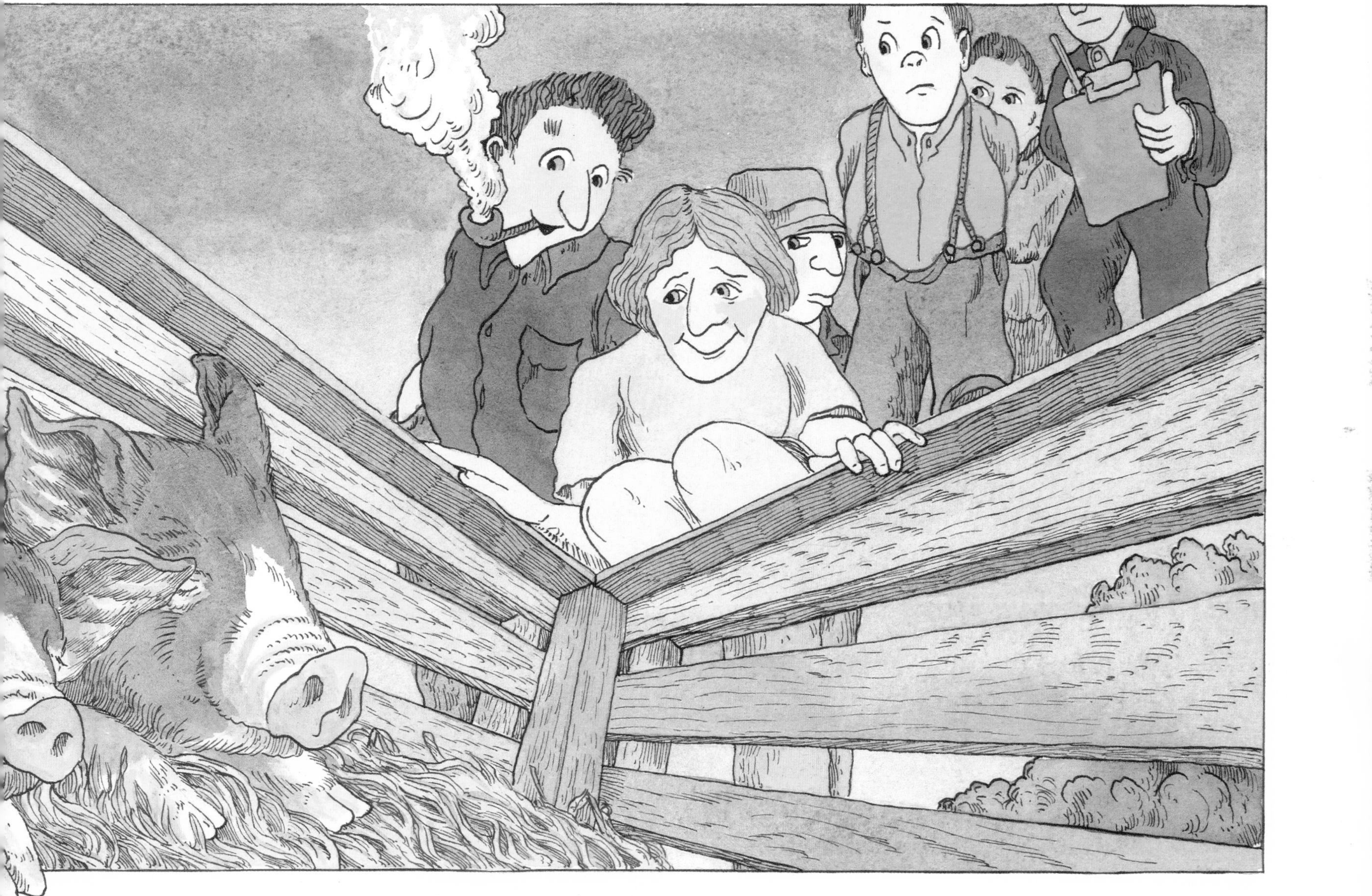

Unhappily, Sid and Olive Cornstalk didn't tell anyone that one of their purchases was not a pig.

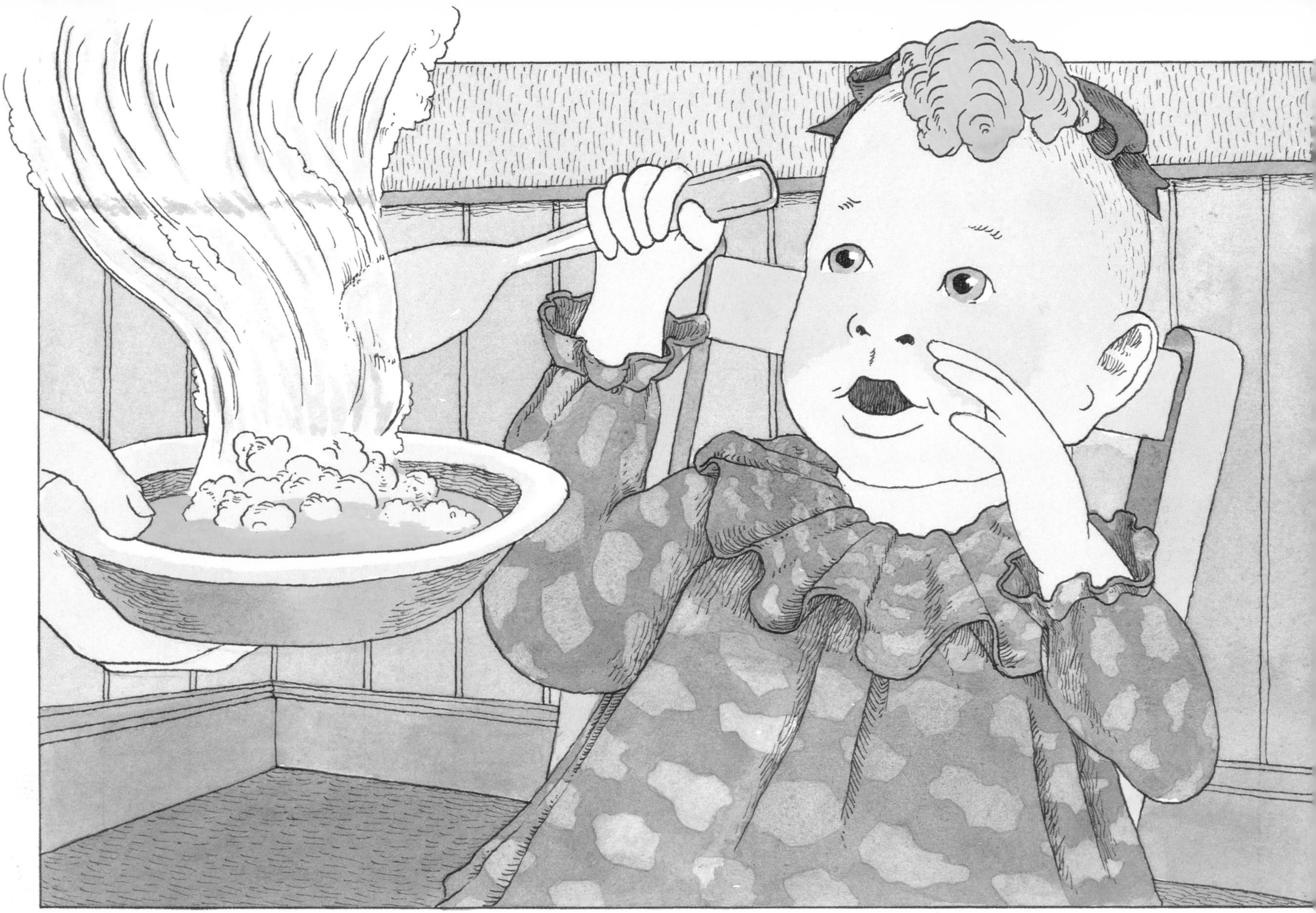

Happily, they took the baby home, scrubbed her till she shone, dressed her in a pretty little dress and gave her real baby food to eat: stewed apple and runny custard.

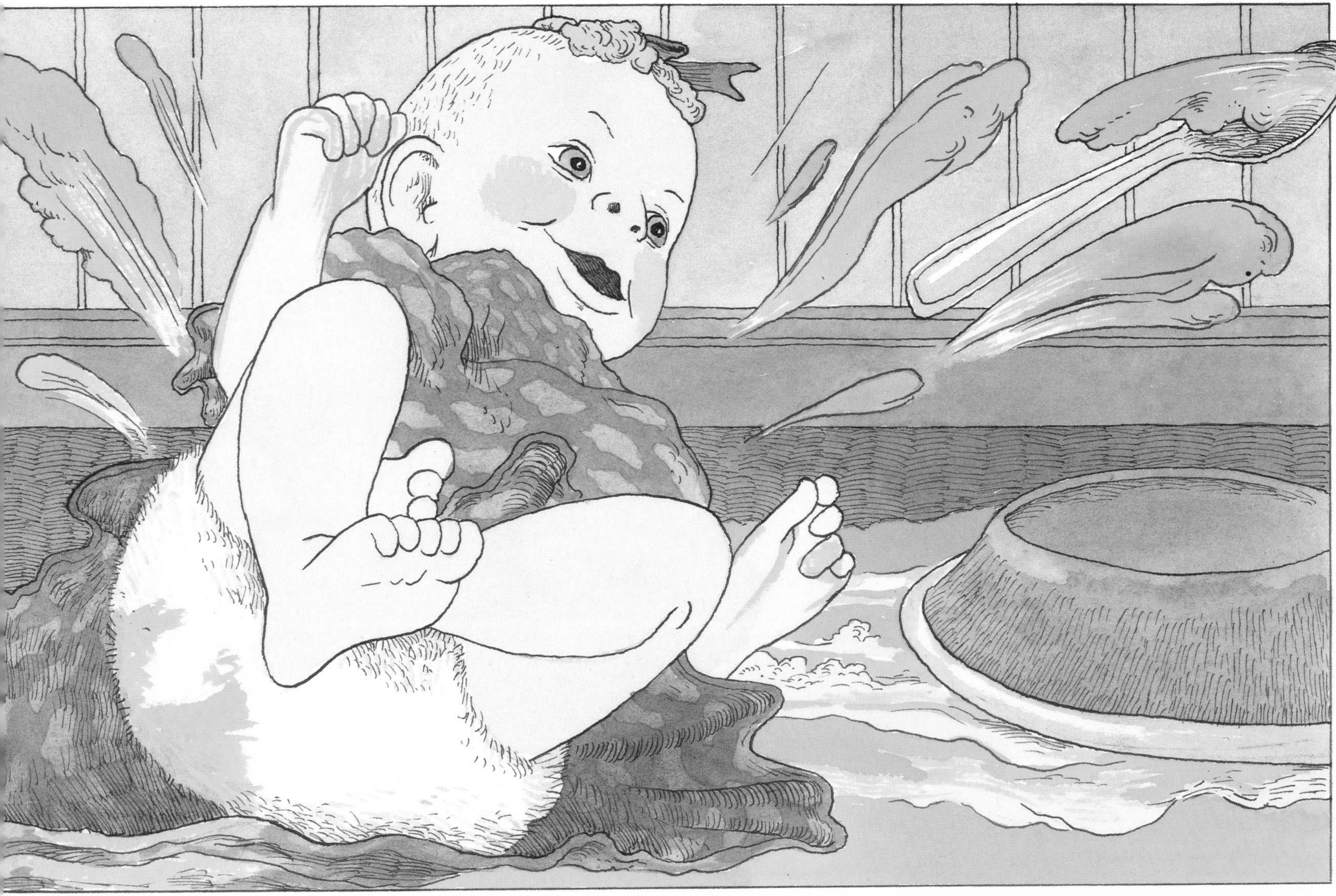

Unhappily, the baby threw the real baby food on the floor and rolled in it, making loud snorting noises and ruining her nice new clothes.

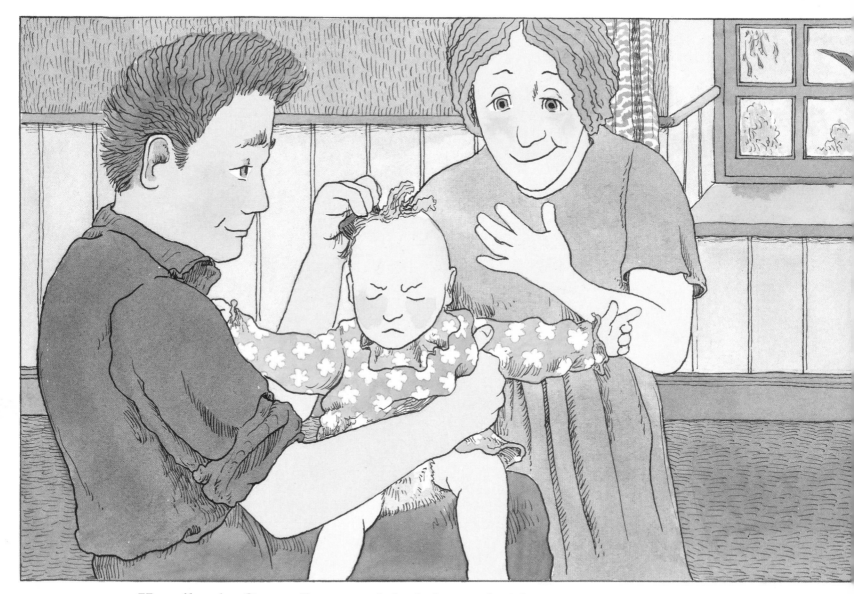

Happily, the Cornstalks rescued the baby, washed her down, and dressed her in another pretty little dress.

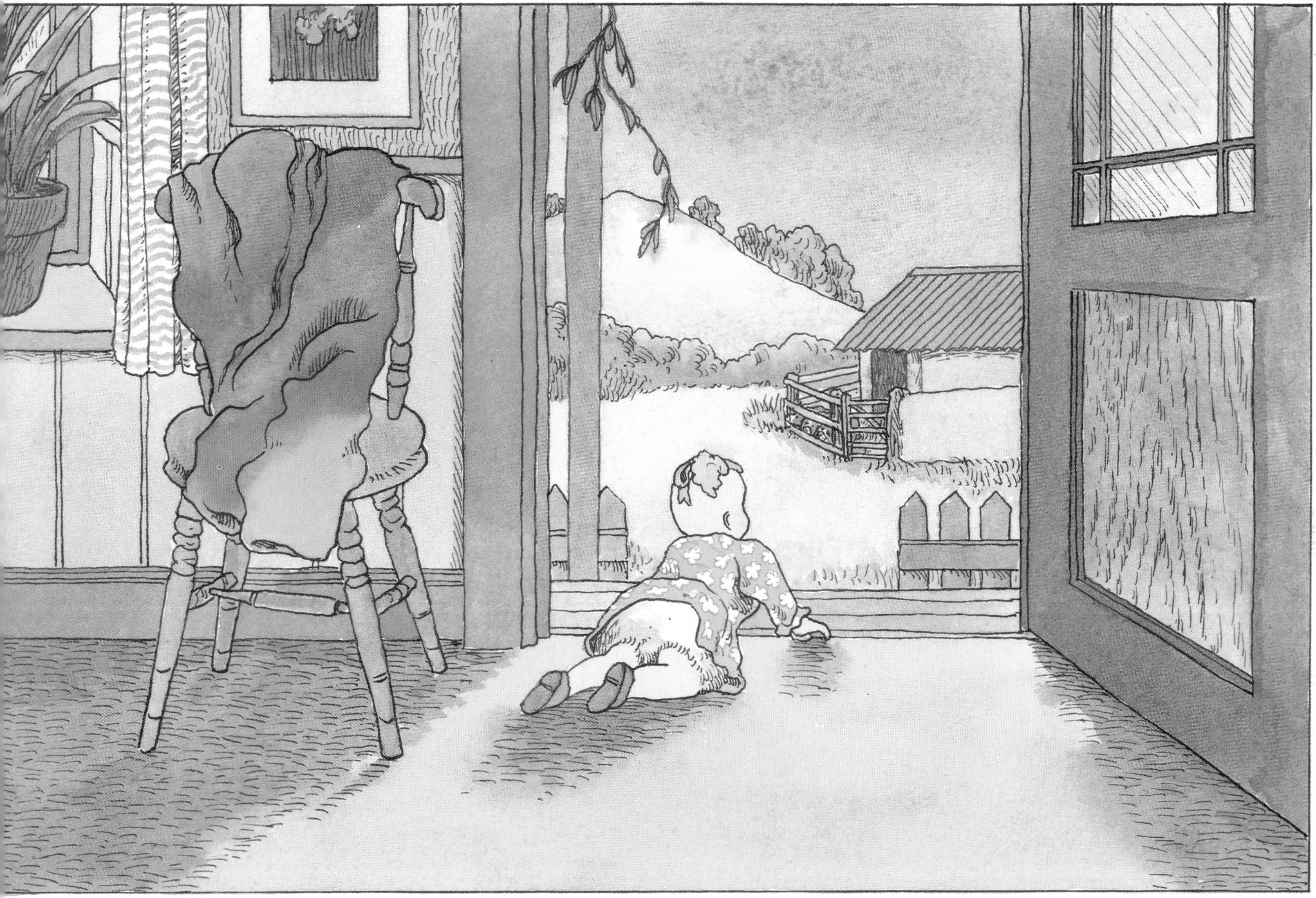

Unhappily, the baby escaped out of the back door and set off at a trot in the direction of the pigsty.

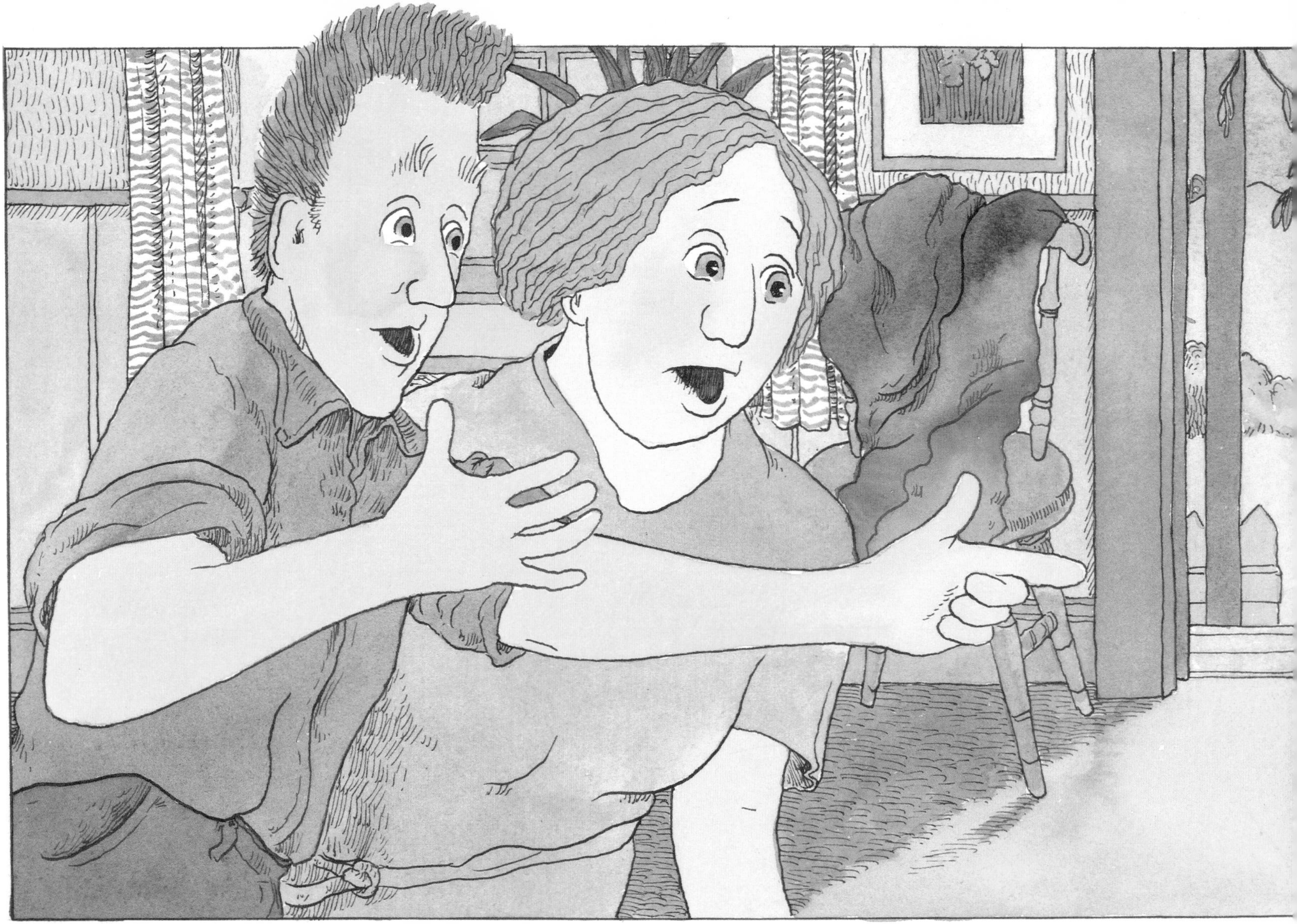

Happily, Sid and Olive Cornstalk, who were patient and persistent people, rushed to recapture the baby.

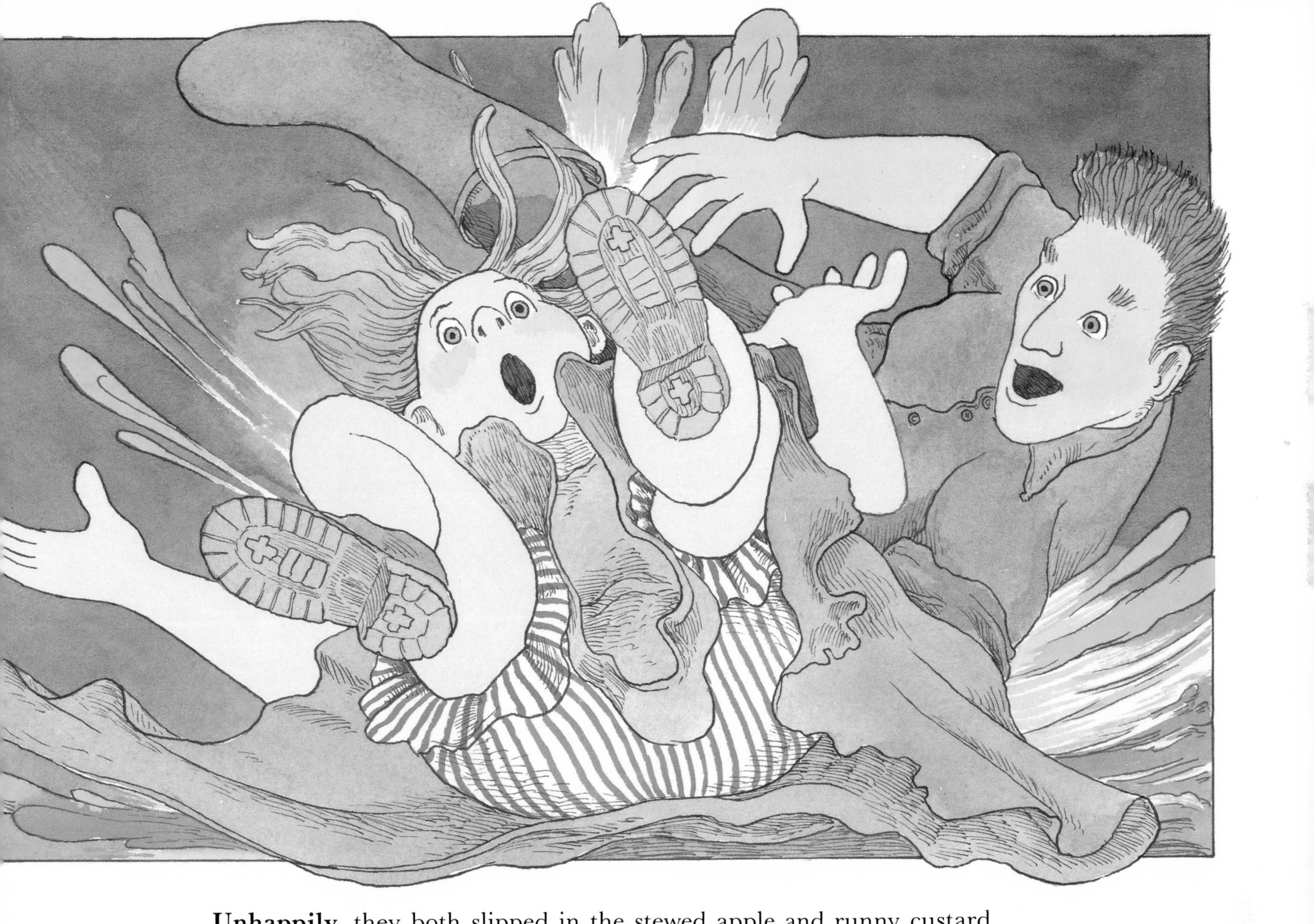

Unhappily, they both slipped in the stewed apple and runny custard.

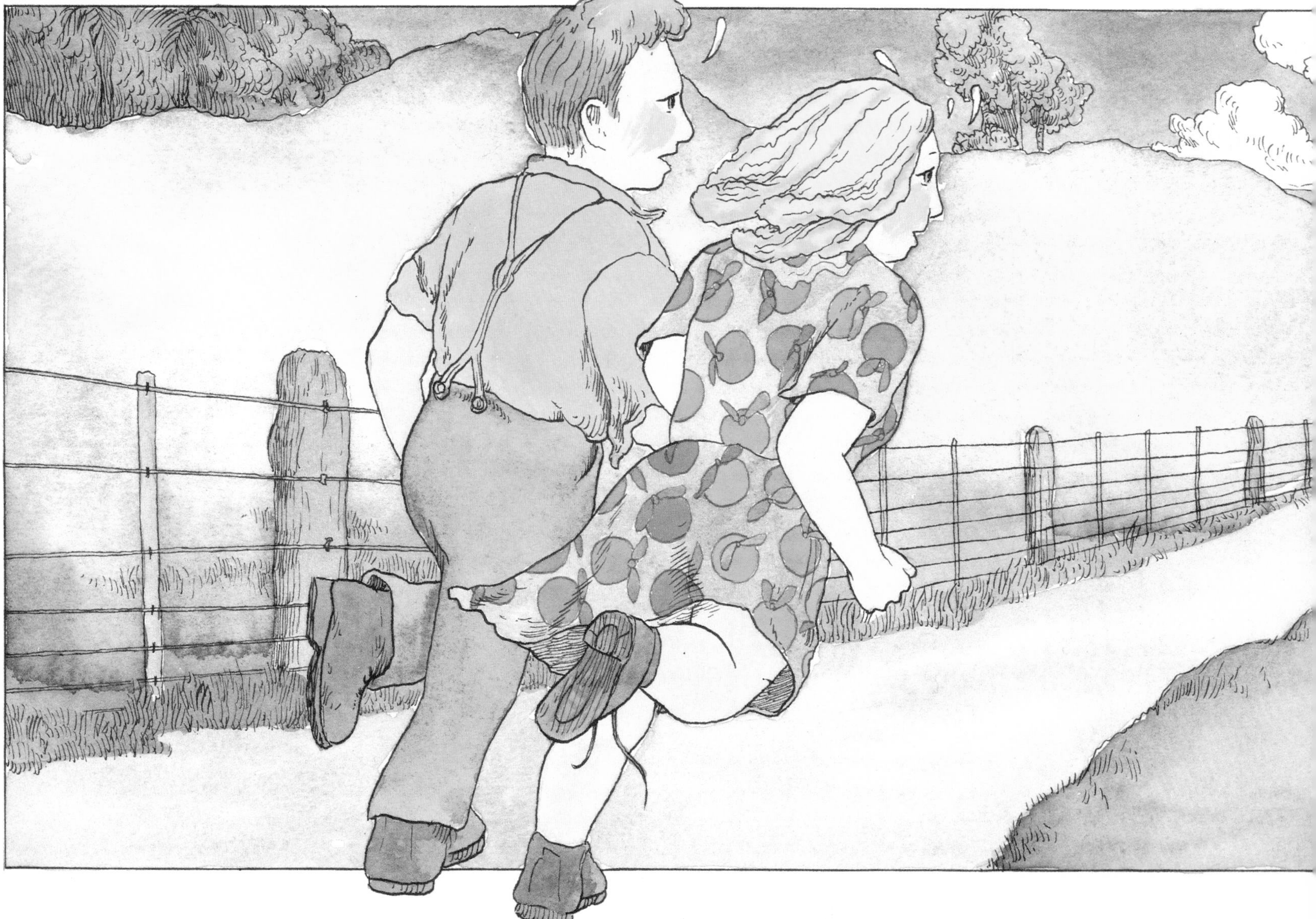

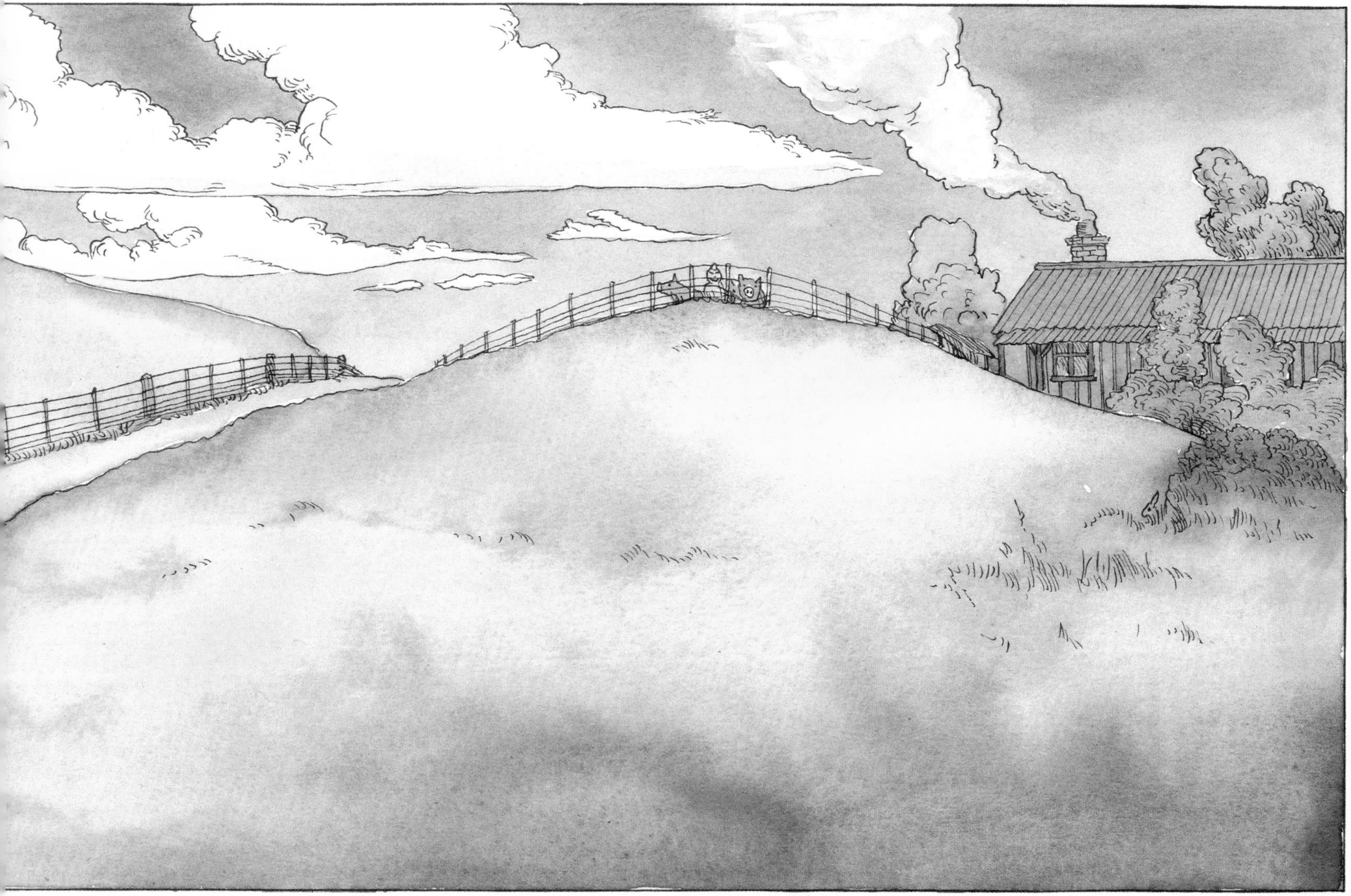

Happily, Mabel and Ned, who were rushing up the road at that very moment shouting, "Baby! Baby! Where are you?", caught sight of the baby over the fence.

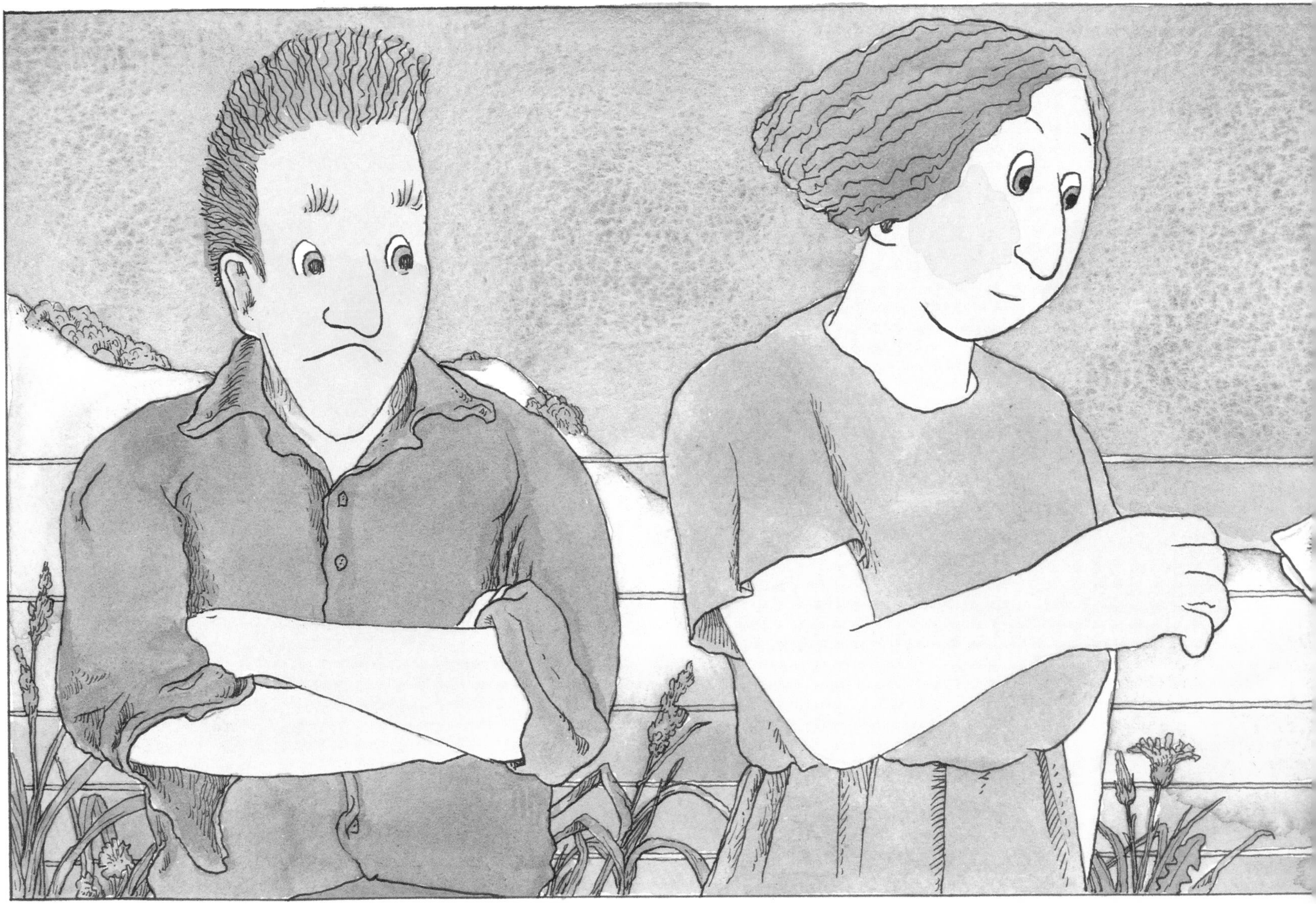

Unhappily, an argument broke out about who really owned the baby, and Mabel and Ned were obliged to pay the price of a new pig to get her back.

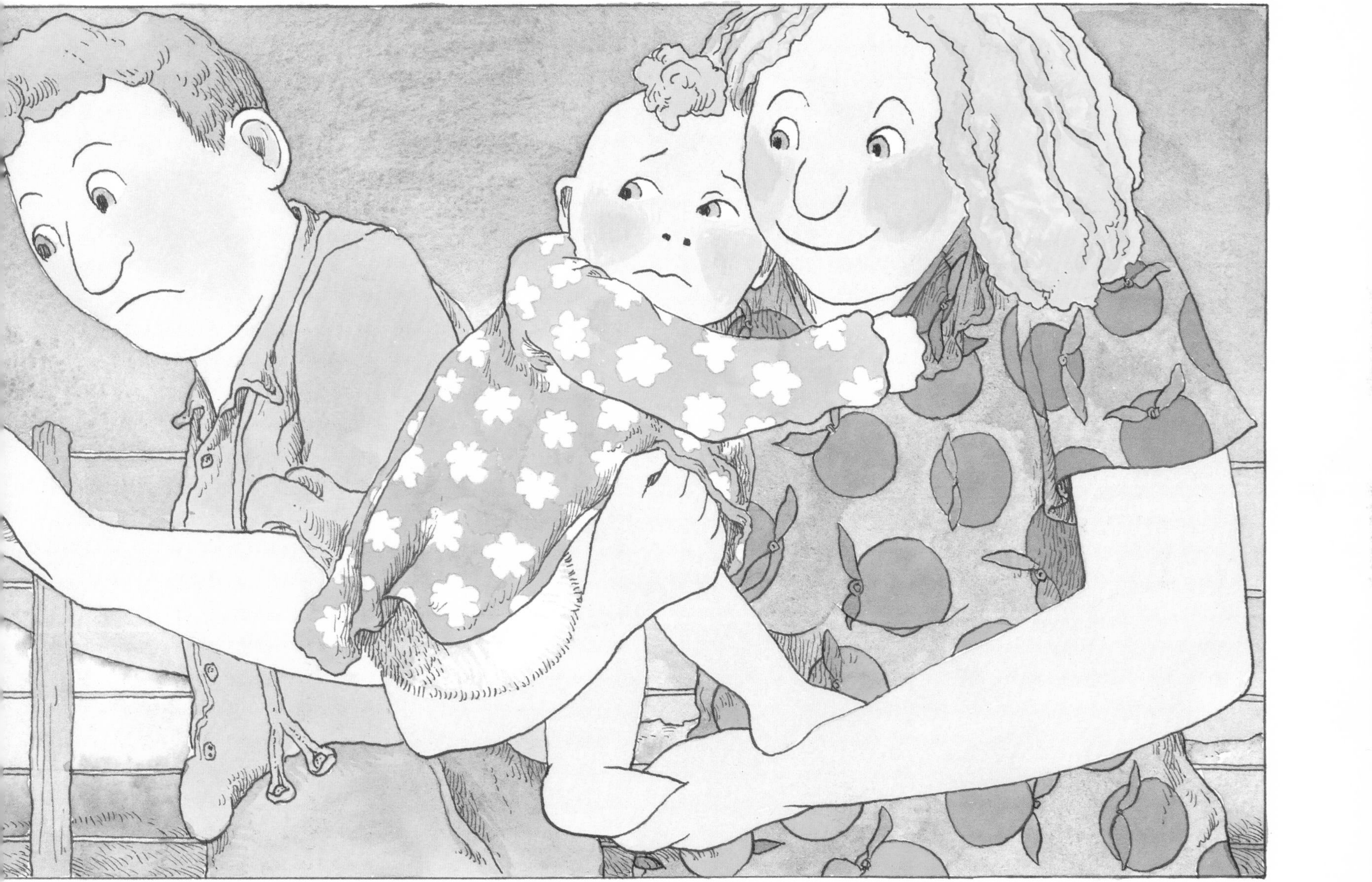

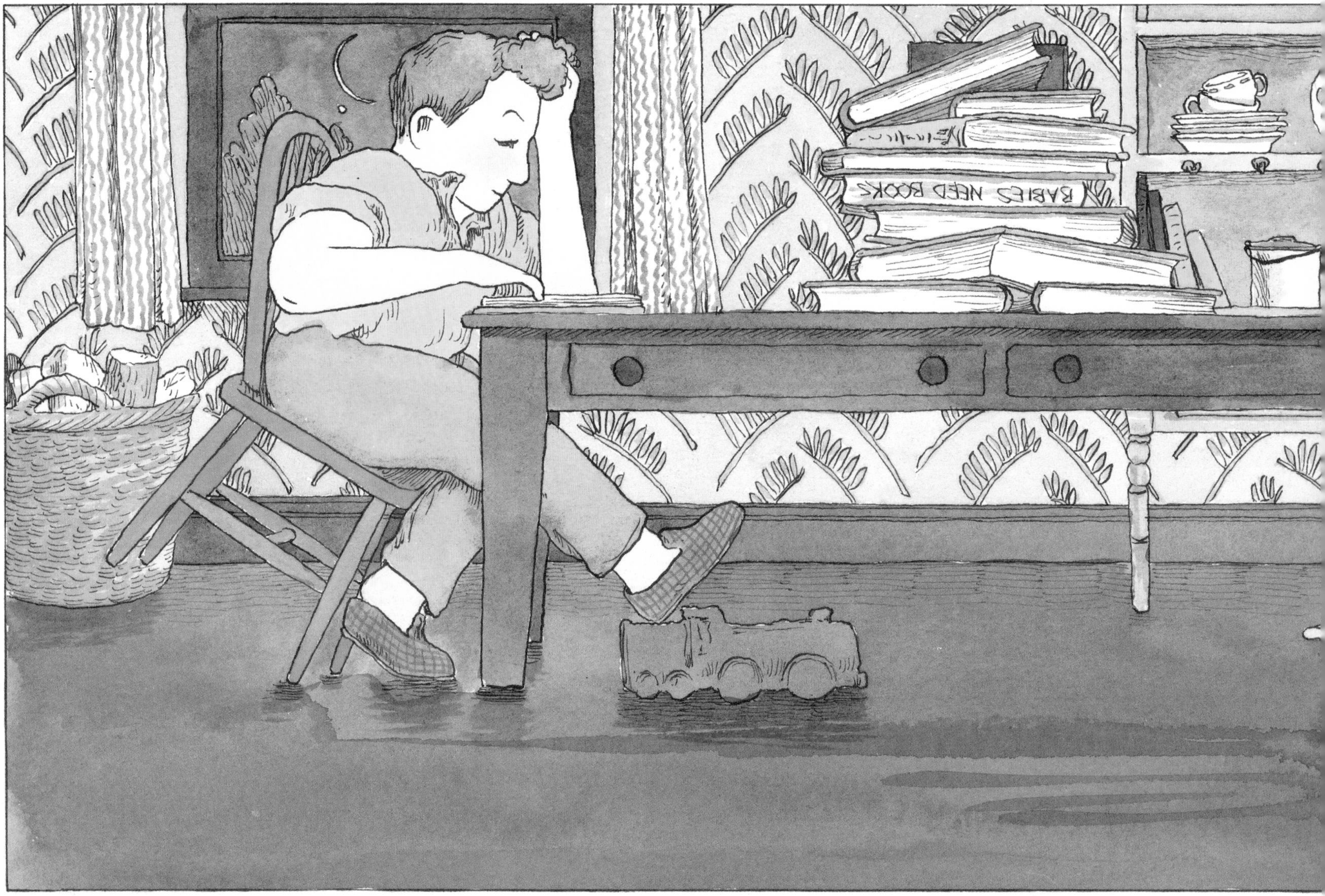
BABIES NEED BOOKS

Happily, Mabel and Ned vowed to be better parents. They joined the library and borrowed a book called *How to Bring up Babies.*

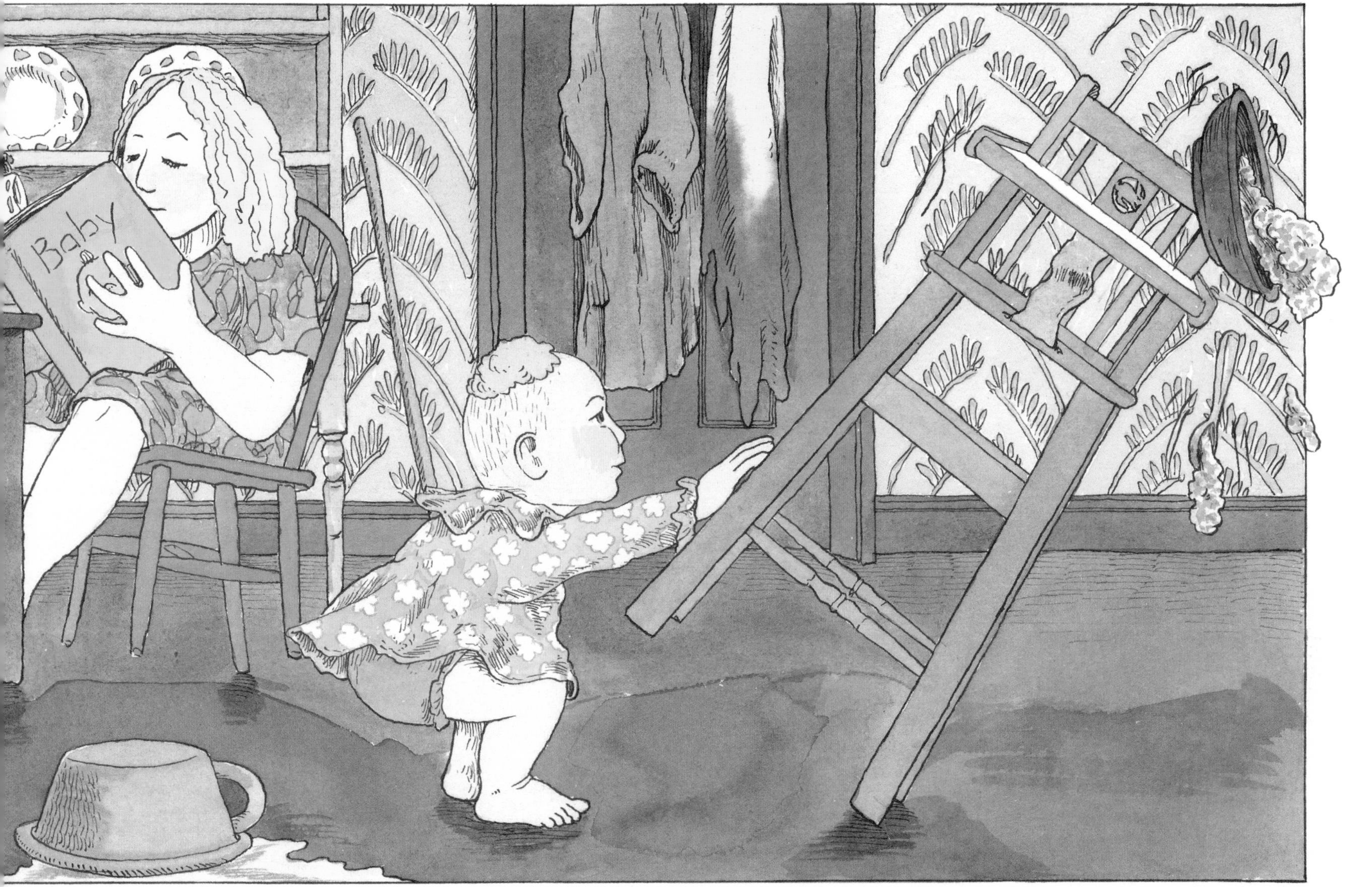
Baby

Unhappily, the baby did not like pretty dresses, high chairs, potties, and mashed vegetables.

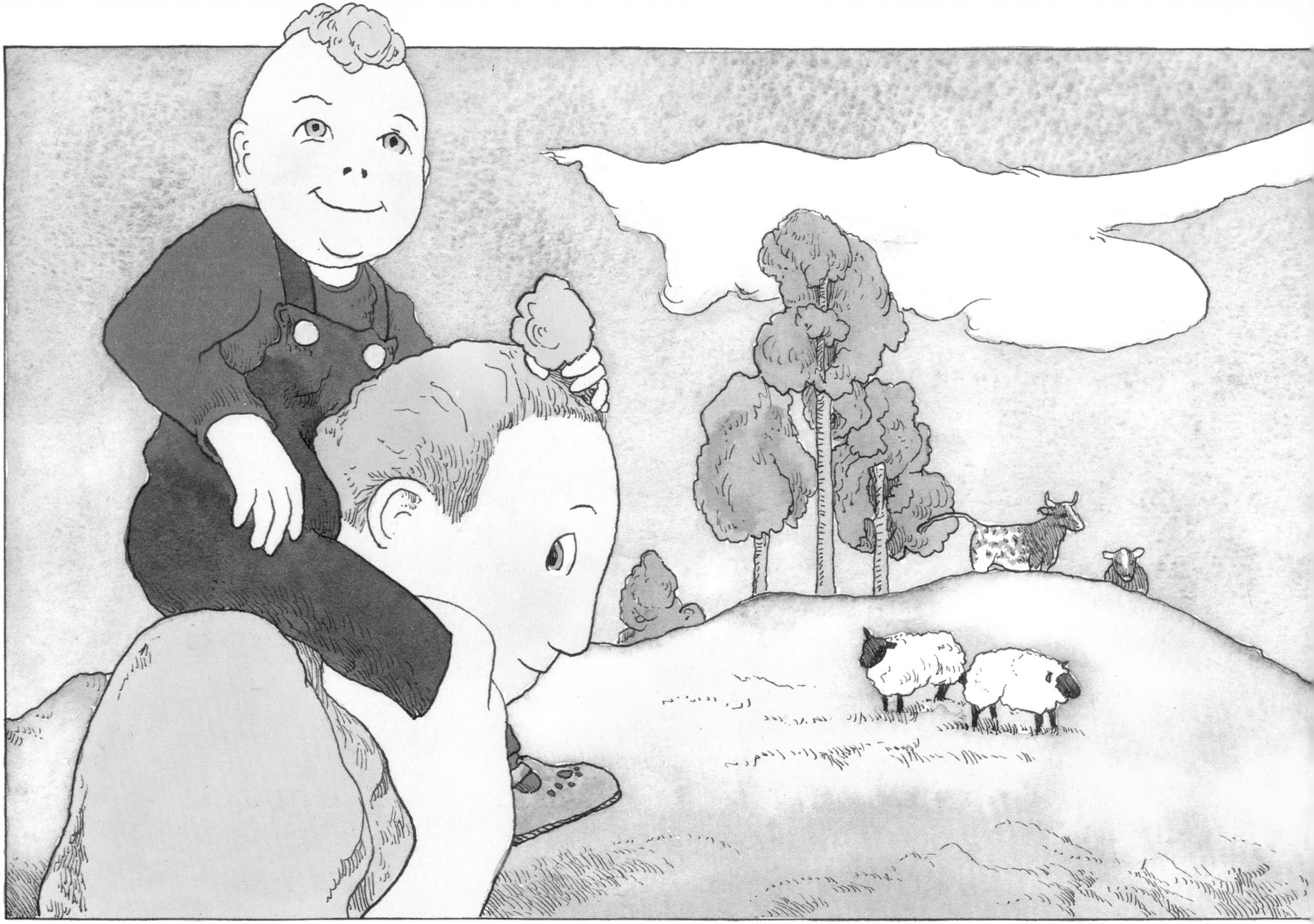

Happily, the baby *did* like overalls, nursery rhymes, riding on Ned's back, and mashed bananas.

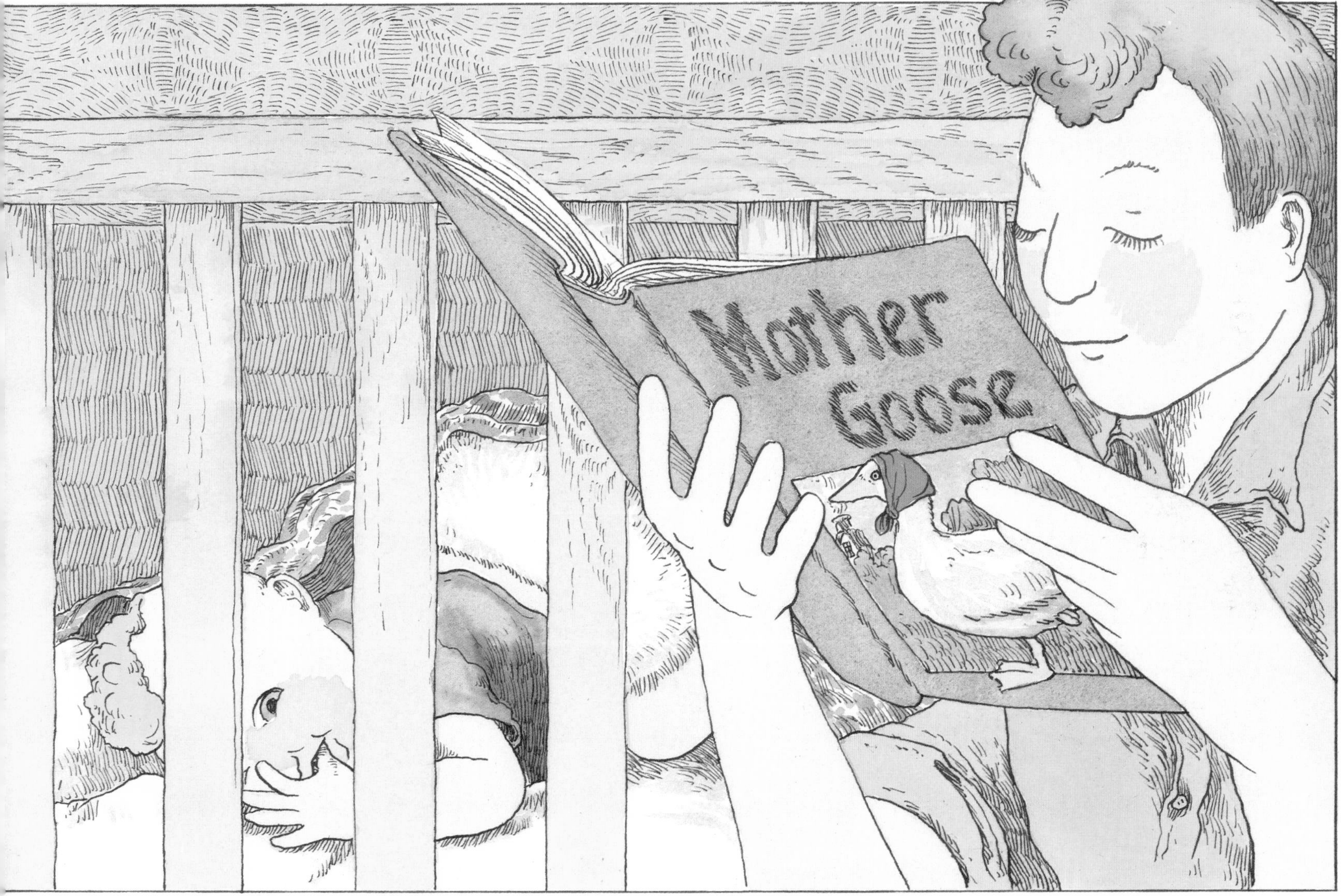
Mother
Goose

Unhappily, the baby still missed her friends the pigs, and cried every night, despite the nursery rhymes.

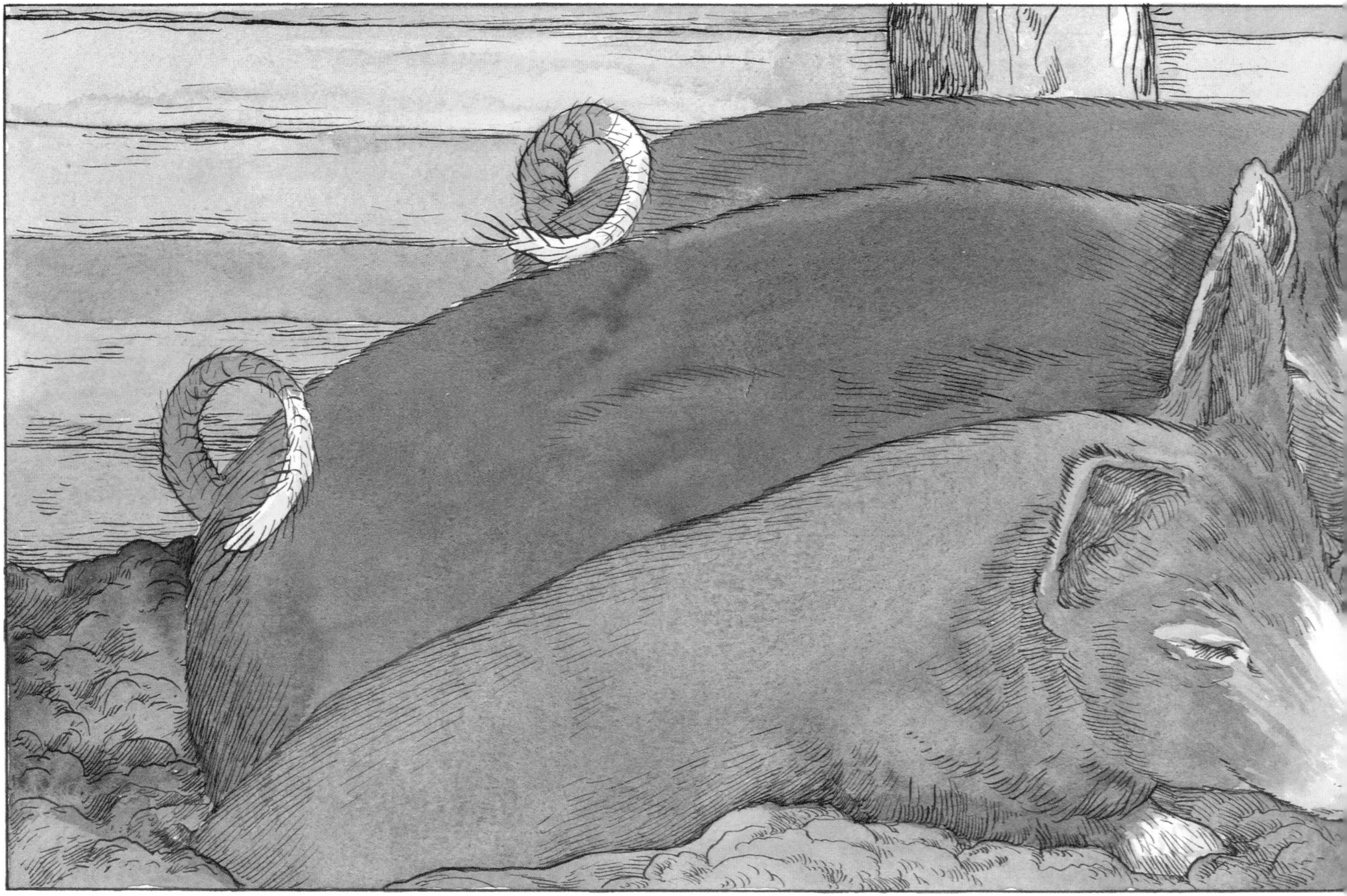

Happily, Mabel and Ned had a bright idea. They let the baby play with the pigs every morning for half an hour just before her bath, so the story ended . . .

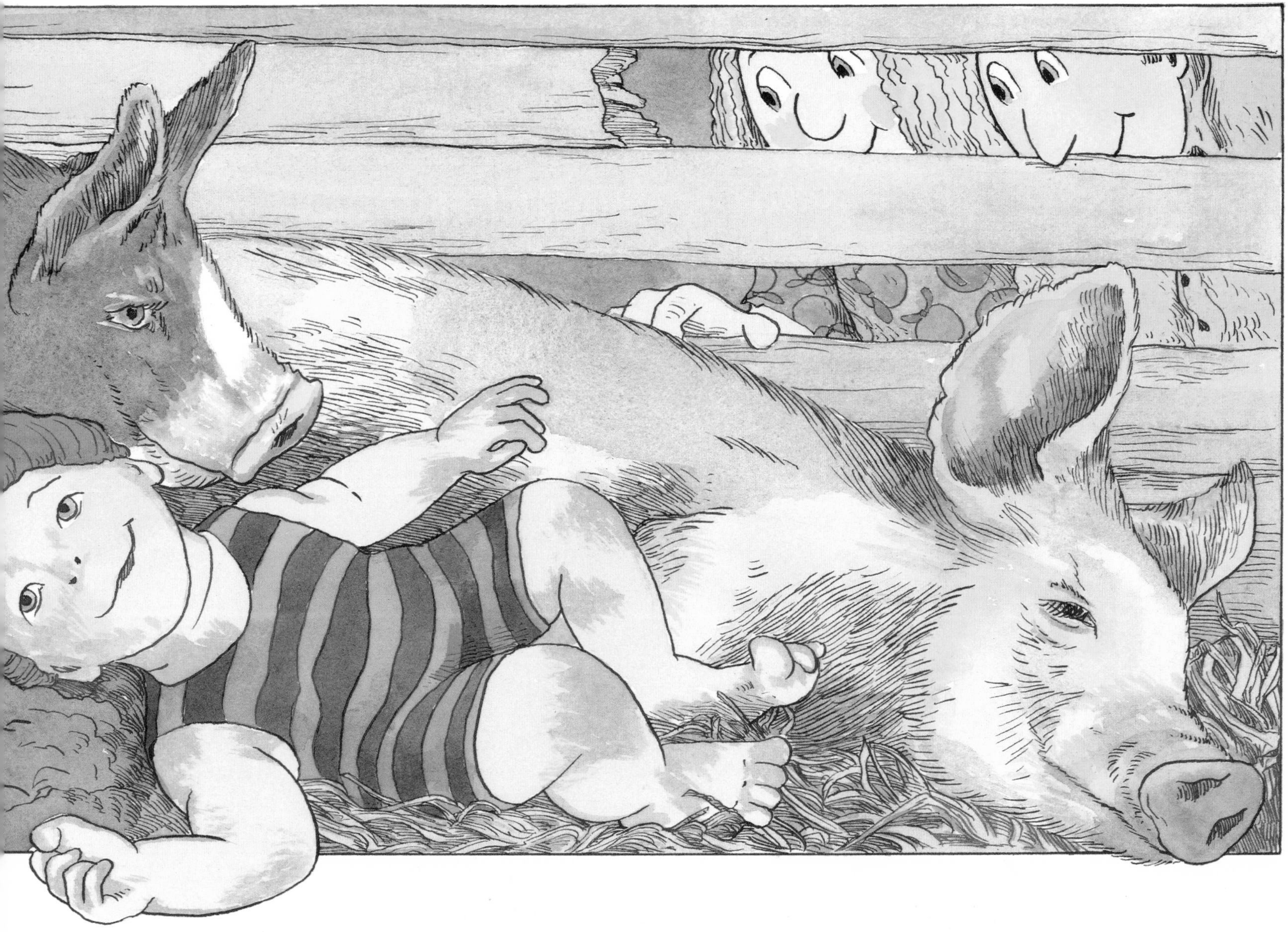

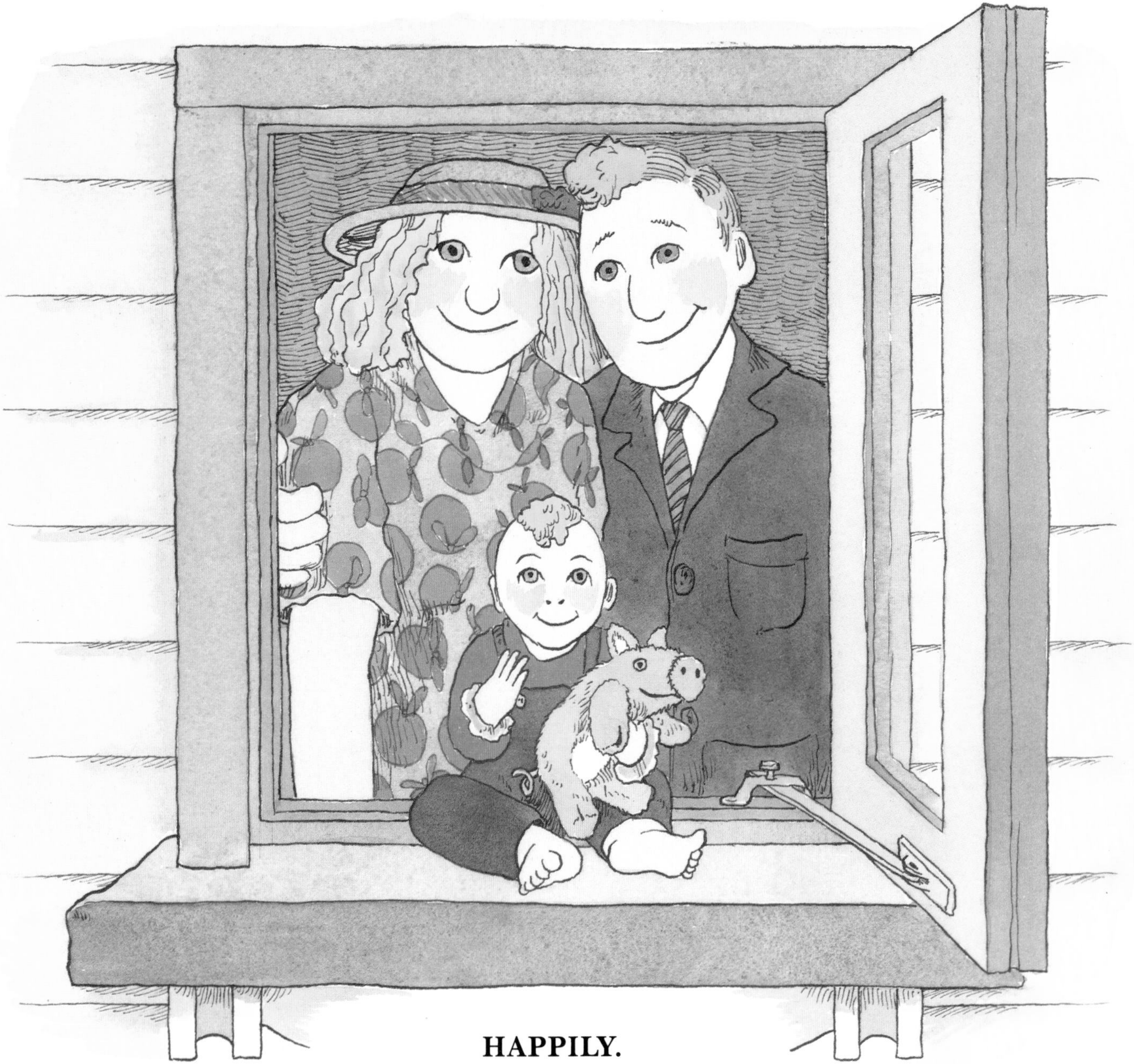

HAPPILY.